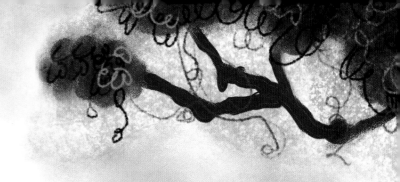

•••TO
MY THREE SONS;
SOUL REBEL, SKIP AND
SAIYAN, YOU ARE MY EVERY-
THING EVERY DAY. AND FOR BOBBY,
OUR VERY SPECIAL CHOCOLATE LAB
WHO BROUGHT US SO MUCH LOVE.
— CEDELLA MARLEY

•••TO
HASHEM AND FOR
MY COMMUNITY WITH
WHOM I SHARE ONE LOVE:
RAY, COY, LORI, ERIC, LORDEAN,
ILENE, AND YVONNE. THANKS FOR
THE LOVE AND PRAYERS, NESTER.
—VANESSA BRANTLEY-NEWTON

• • •

Library of Congress Cataloging-in-Publication Data
Marley, Cedella.
One love / by Cedella Marley ; illustrated by Vanessa
Brantley-Newton.
p. cm.
"Based on the song by Bob Marley."
Summary: In this illustrated version of Bob Marley's
song, a young girl enlists her friends, family, and
community to transform their neighborhood for
the better.
ISBN-13: 978-1-4521-0224-5 (alk. paper)
ISBN-10: 1-4521-0224-4
1. Children's songs—Texts. 2. Picture
books for children. [1. Love—Songs
and music. 2. Songs.] I. Brantley-
Newton, Vanessa, ill. II. Marley,
Bob. One love. III. Title.
PZ8.3.M39178
782.42—dc22
2010052635

Book design by Kristine Brogno.
Typeset in Family Cat, Family Cat Fat,
and Gotham.

• • •

The illustrations in this book were rendered
in mixed media and digitally.

• • •

Manufactured by Toppan Leefung, Da Ling
Shan Town, Dongguan, China, in September 2016.

• • •

20 19 18 17 16 15 14 13 12 11

• • •

This product conforms to CPSIA 2008.

• • •

Chronicle Books LLC
680 Second Street
San Francisco, California
94107

• • •

www.chroniclekids.com

TUFF
GONG™

BASED ON THE SONG BY
BOB MARLEY
ONE
LOVE

adapted by **Cedella Marley** ♥ illustrated by Vanessa Brantley-Newton

chronicle books · san francisco

One love,
one heart,
let's get together
and feel all right!

One love,
what my family
gives to me.

One love,

what the flower
gives the bee.

One love,

what Mother Earth
gives the tree.

One love,
one heart,

let's get together and feel all right!

One heart,
    like the birds,
 I long to be free.

One love,
like the river
runs to the sea.

One heart,

like the music,
    just feel the beat.

Let's get together and feel all right!

One love,
        when your hand
reaches out for me.

One heart, when we touch,

a new world we'll see.

One love, one heart,

let's get together and feel all right!

"One love, one heart, let's get together and feel all right."

Simple and true—but it seems to be the hardest thing to do. From my parents' humble beginnings in Jamaica's Trench Town, the one thing they always instilled in us was, and still is, love.

My father once said, "Children is wonderful, a part of my richness." The richness was not monetary but rather the joy he felt in his heart when he looked upon his children. I feel the same thing every time I look at my three boys. So when I started to adapt his song "One Love" as the basis for this picture book, I knew, at once, it would be a heartfelt project.

I think everybody has a "happy song" and "One Love" is mine. Yet, in many ways, it's everybody's happy song. It's also a healing song, and I played it for my boys when they weren't feeling well. "One Love" is also a great "sleepy time song." I remember humming it softly as I cuddled with my boys on those nights when nothing else worked for them . . . or me.

When my father sang "One Love," he felt it all the way—heart and soul, mind and body. He thought a world united by love was possible, and it is. All we've got to do, he said, is "Give a little, take a little." My father wanted people to embrace one another and take care of one another. That was and is the message of "One Love." And I have tried to pass that message of love and community to all of the readers of this book.

I hope "One Love" will be your "happy-healing-sleepy" song because I know it can do for you what it has always done for me and my kids.

One love to everyone!

Cedella Marley